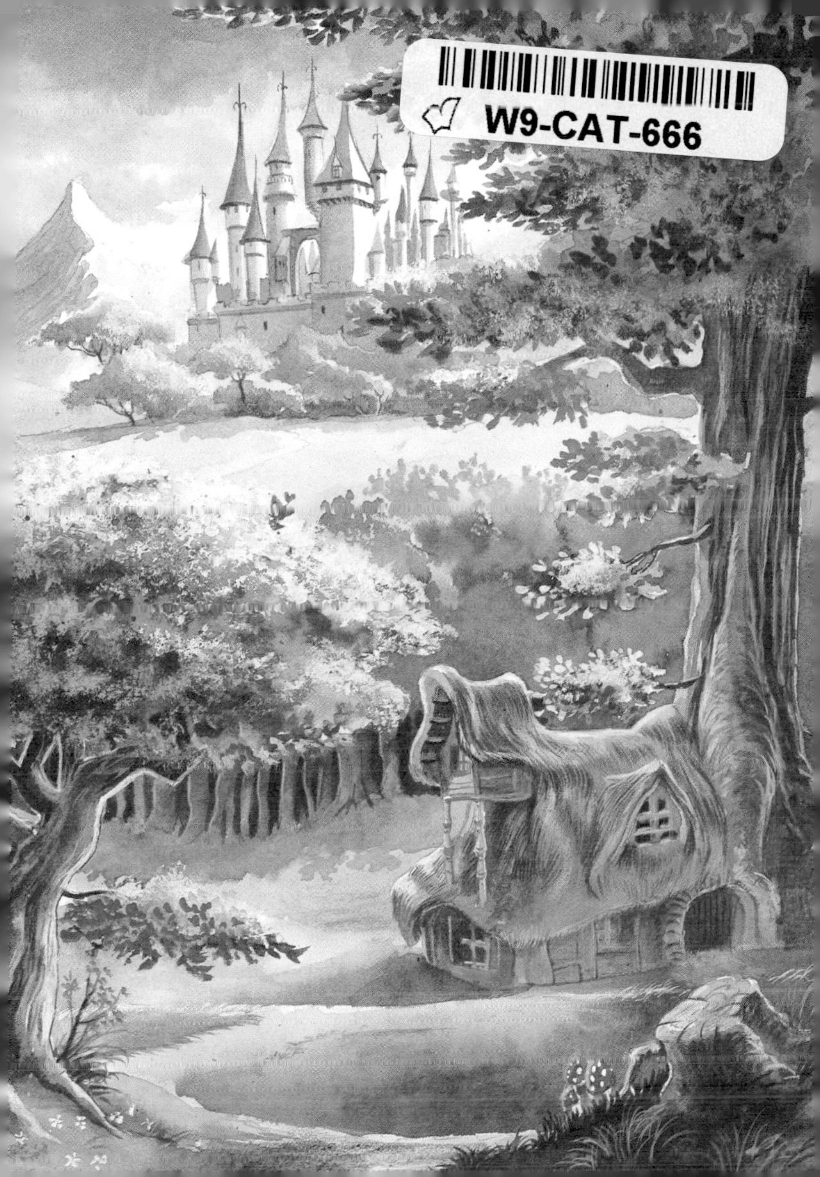

Graphic design and illustrations: Zapp
Story adaptation: Robyn Bryant

© 1995 Tormont Publications Inc.
   338 Saint Antoine St. East
   Montreal, Canada H2Y 1A3
   Tel. (514) 954-1441
   Fax (514) 954-5086

ISBN 2-89429-841-2

Printed in China

CINDERELLA

TORMONT

Once upon a time, there was a girl named Ella. Her mother was very ill. One day, she called Ella to her bedside. "Ella, I am leaving this world," she whispered. "But I will always watch over you like a little dove sitting on your shoulder."

After she died, Ella's father, a sea captain, married the Widow Javotte. Madame Javotte was mean, and her daughters, Gertrude and Hortense, were spoiled and selfish.

All three were jealous of Ella's sweet nature and her beauty. So they took away her fine dresses, and made her work like a servant.

All day, she cooked and scrubbed. And at night, she had to sleep on a straw mat by the kitchen fire among the cinders. They called her Cinderella.

"Cinderella, get my breakfast!" Hortense yelled.

"Cinderella, polish my shoes!" Gertrude shouted.

Yet she never complained, not even to her father during the few days he came home from sea each year.

One day, the family received an invitation to a ball at the palace. The King's son was looking for a wife!

"I'm sure the Prince will choose me," Hortense announced.

"You? You're too ugly!" cried Gertrude. And they argued until their mother stopped them.

Poor Cinderella worked even harder getting her sisters ready for the ball. She sewed their hems and combed their hair. She starched their crinolines and polished their jewels.

Cinderella quietly asked if she could go to the ball, too. Her sisters only laughed.

Her stepmother said nothing.
Instead, she went to the kitchen
and grabbed a big bag of lentils.
Then she emptied the whole bag
into the ashes in the fireplace.

"You may come to the ball,
Cinderella, after you pick up every
lentil!" she said.

When her stepmother left the kitchen, Cinderella raced to the window and called her friends the birds. The birds loved Cinderella because she fed them every day. They hopped into the kitchen and helped her pick up every lentil.

But when Cinderella showed her stepmother the lentils, Madame said, "Lentils or no, you are not going to the ball. You are filthy and ragged. Your place is by the fire — not at a party with fine ladies in satin."

Then, without another word, Madame
and her daughters climbed into their
carriage and sped off to the ball, leaving
poor Cinderella crying by the fireplace.

Suddenly, in a swirl of blue light, a Fairy appeared. "Don't cry, Cinderella," the Fairy said. "You shall go to the ball, no matter what anyone says. Now hurry to the garden and bring me a pumpkin, six mice, and a fat rat."

Cinderella soon found everything on the list. The Fairy tapped the pumpkin with her wand. Presto! It sprouted into a magnificent carriage! The six mice were transformed into fine white horses. And the rat became a handsome coachman.

"Now for a gown," said the Fairy. Her
magic wand wrapped Cinderella in a dress
made of pale silver and gold threads.
Crystal earrings and a rose adorned
her hair. With one last tap of her wand,
delicate glass slippers appeared on
Cinderella's feet.

"You must remember one thing, my child. You must leave the ball at midnight. When the clock finishes striking twelve, the spell will end. The coach will turn back into a pumpkin, and you will be dressed in rags once again."

"I'll remember," Cinderella said.

When Cinderella entered the ballroom, the guests were struck silent by her beauty.

"Who could she be?" everyone whispered.

Even Cinderella's stepsisters curtsied before her, thinking she was foreign royalty.

The Prince had eyes only for Cinderella.
"I've never seen you before. Tell me who
you are," he begged her.

"It's not important," she replied. "But
it's true we haven't met before." And she
smiled at him so radiantly that he did not
pry any further.

That evening, the Prince danced only with Cinderella. By midnight, he had fallen completely in love with her.

Cinderella was so happy that she forgot about the time. Only when the clock began to strike twelve did she remember the Fairy's warning.

Without a word to the Prince, she ran from the ballroom. She lost one of her slippers on the stairs, but there was no time to pick it up.

Cinderella kept running until she realized she was in rags again, with the mice and rat scurrying along beside her.

The Prince chased after Cinderella, but
she had disappeared. He found only her
glass slipper on the stairs.

He took the slipper to the King.
"Father, I plan to marry the girl whose
foot fits this slipper," he announced. "Will
you help me find her?"

The next morning, Cinderella's sisters could talk of nothing but the ball.

"You should have seen it, Cinderella. A beautiful stranger showed up, and the Prince danced only with her," Gertrude said.

"But then she ran off without a word, and lost her slipper," Hortense added.

"Now the Prince says he will marry whoever fits the shoe!" Gertrude cried. "How difficult can that be? It's only a shoe!"

But it was very difficult indeed. The Prince traveled throughout the kingdom, and hundreds of women tried on the glass slipper. But no one could fit into it perfectly. Finally, the Prince arrived at Cinderella's house.

First Hortense, and then Gertrude, tried to cram a foot into the glass slipper, without success.

"May I try it on?" Cinderella asked shyly.

"His Royal Highness does not have time to waste," her stepmother said.

"It's no bother," the Prince said. He slid the glass slipper onto Cinderella's foot. It fit perfectly!

"But she was not even at the ball last night!" her sisters cried. Cinderella simply pulled out the other slipper from her pocket. "It really is you," the Prince whispered.

The Prince led Cinderella away to his castle. They were married a week later. At the wedding, a dove appeared and touched Cinderella on her shoulder. "Your mother says that you will live happily ever after," it whispered.

And indeed she did!